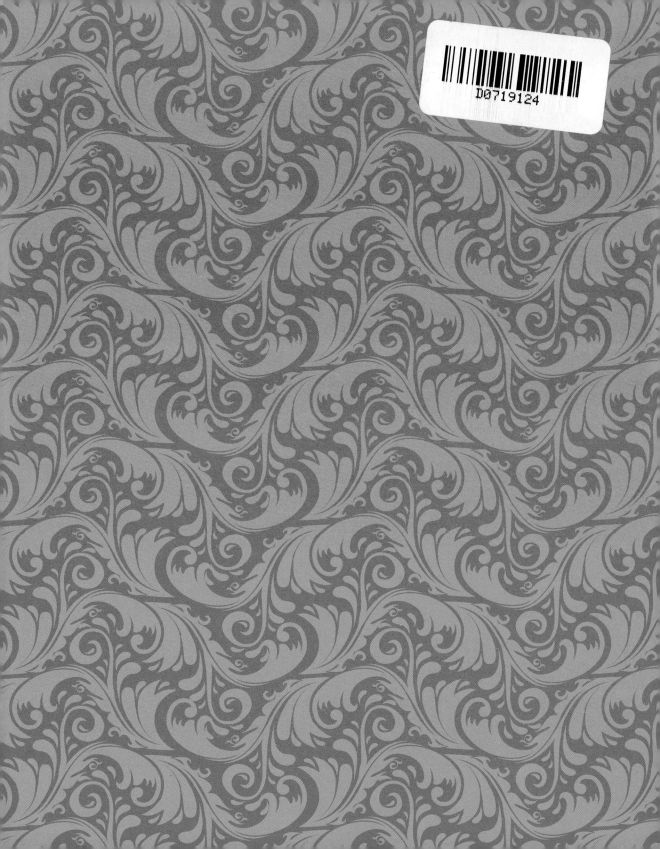

This igloo book belongs to:

....

Contents

Published in 2015
by Igloo Books Ltd
Cottage Farm
Sywell
NN6 0BJ
www.igloobooks.com

LEO002 1214
2 4 6 8 10 9 7 5 3 1
ISBN: 978-1-78440-179-5

Illustrated by Amanda Enright

Printed and manufactured in China

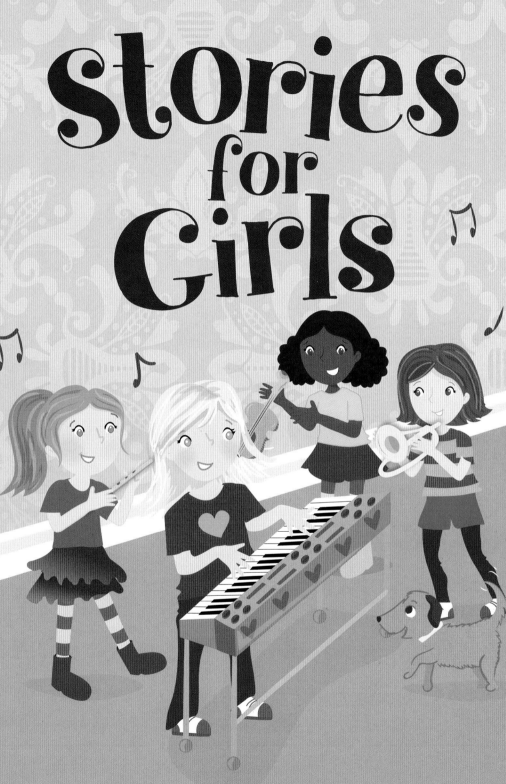

stories
for
Girls

igloobooks

Poppy's Puppy

Poppy was very happy indeed. She had wanted a puppy for ages and at last, Dad had brought one home for her. He was brown with a white eye patch and Poppy decided to call him Scamp. Poppy held Scamp gently and took him upstairs. "Look, Mum," she said. "The puppy's here."

Poppy's mum was busy looking for something. "I've lost my wedding ring," she said. Mum looked at Scamp. "He's very cute, Poppy, but please make sure he behaves. I don't want anything else going missing."
"Yes, Mum," said Poppy, feeling a bit disappointed that Mum didn't seem to like Scamp.

Poppy decided to take Scamp out into the garden, but he wanted to explore his new home. He wriggled out of Poppy's arms and dashed off downstairs, knocking over the coat stand as he ran. Hats, coats and scarves went flying everywhere. "Stop, Scamp!" cried Poppy, trying to grab him, but he dashed into the living room.

Scamp jumped onto the sofa, scattering cushions everywhere, then he raced around the room in excitement. He bumped into the coffee table and knocked over a lamp, then he yapped and dived for Dad's feet. So, Dad toppled over onto the sofa. "Scamp, that's very naughty. Come here," gasped Poppy, but Scamp was already heading for the kitchen.

Scamp slid all over the clean, kitchen floor. He tipped over the mop and bucket, crashed into Mum's shopping bags and toppled the rubbish bin, spilling rubbish all over the floor. "Come here, you naughty puppy," said Poppy, as Scamp began sniffing at something. She was worried that Mum and Dad would be cross.

Just then, Mum and Dad came into the kitchen and stared at the mess Scamp had made. Mum stood with her hands on her hips and Dad crossed his arms. Neither of Poppy's parents looked happy. "I'm going to get told off," thought Poppy, but then something strange happened.

Suddenly, Mum began to smile. She was staring at the rubbish
bin that Scamp had knocked over. In among the cans and banana
skins, something was glinting. "It's my wedding ring!" she cried.
"Scamp found it. What a clever puppy."

Mum picked Scamp up and hugged him. Dad laughed as
Scamp licked her face and Poppy was thrilled. "It looks like
Scamp is going to be the perfect pet for us," said Poppy.
"I think he is," said Mum, giving Poppy a big hug.
Scamp wagged his tail and barked in agreement.

The Hide-and-Seek Hamster

Maisy was panicking. It was only three days since she'd brought home her new hamster, Charlie and now he had gone missing. "I promised the lady at the pet shop I'd take good care of him," she said, as she looked at the empty cage. "Now I've lost him."

Maisy looked around her bedroom. There were so many places a little hamster could hide. She looked under the bed, in her wardrobe and behind her pile of toys. Maisy even looked inside all her socks, but Charlie was nowhere to be seen.

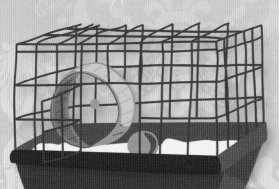

Maisy rushed out onto the landing and bumped into her
brother, Ollie. "I've lost Charlie," she sobbed.
"Don't worry," said Ollie. "I'll help you look." So, they went
into the bathroom and searched in the bath and even down
the toilet! Charlie was nowhere to be seen.

"Maybe he managed to get downstairs," said Maisy.
So, Maisy and Ollie checked the staircase, then they looked
in the hall and the kitchen, where their mum offered to help
them look. "I hope Charlie's not scared," Maisy said, sadly.

When Dad came in from the garden, they told him what was happening and he eagerly joined in the hamster hunt.
He crawled around on his hands and knees looking for hamster paw prints, but all he found was a missing button. Mum looked everywhere, too, but Charlie was still nowhere to be found.

Before long, the entire house had been turned upside down,
as the family searched for Charlie. Drawers and cupboards had
been emptied. Shelves had been cleared. Even the plant pots
had been searched. Maisy laid on her bed and cried.
"We'll never find him," she said, sadly. "Poor Charlie."

Maisy looked sadly at Charlie's cage. As she did, she saw a little, wiggly nose appear. Soon, whiskers poked out, then two round, black eyes and finally, a furry little body. "Charlie!" cried Maisy with delight. "You were in there the whole time." Maisy picked him up, cuddled him and put him in his exercise ball.

"Hooray," said Dad when he saw Maisy holding Charlie.
"Now we can call off the search." They all watched as Charlie
rolled around in his exercise ball. "I'm glad someone has
some energy," said Dad. "I'm worn out."
"I agree," Mum added. "Next time Charlie wants to play
hide-and-seek, we'll do the hiding!"

The Spotty Pony

"Please can we go and see Sandy?" begged Alice. She had just returned from her holiday with Mum and Dad and couldn't wait to visit the beautiful, spotty pony. Alice spent all her spare time at Evergreen Farm, feeding the goats and collecting eggs, but what she loved most of all was riding Sandy.

When Mum had booked a holiday cottage for the summer, Alice had been upset at the thought of not seeing or riding Sandy for a whole month. "I hope she remembers me," said Alice, grabbing an apple. She ran all the way to the farm but when she got there, the paddock was empty. Sandy had gone.

Alice looked around the field and checked in the stables, but Sandy was nowhere to be seen. As she searched the farmyard, Alice heard a clip-clopping sound coming from the barn. "It's Sandy!" she cried, but it wasn't. It was Buttercup the cow with her new calf.

"How cute," said Alice, but she didn't stroke the calf. She had to find Sandy. Suddenly, Alice heard a snuffling sound. "That must be her," Alice said and she followed the sound to the pig pen, but all she found were piglets snuffling around. She was beginning to wonder if she'd ever see Sandy again.

"Farmer Fred must have moved Sandy to the meadow," said Alice. "She loves grazing there." However, as Alice peered across the meadow, all she could see were fluffy, white sheep and lambs. The lambs were so sweet, Alice couldn't resist playing with them. They made her laugh as they bounced about, but she still had to find Sandy.

Alice thought Sandy really had gone away and she knew the
only way to find out was to ask Farmer Fred. She heard him
whistling in a nearby field. "Hello, Alice," he said, smiling.
"Are you looking for Sandy?" Alice nodded. "She's in the far
field," he told her. "Sandy has got a little surprise for you."

Alice ran off as fast as she could to the far field. At first glance, the field looked completely empty. Alice was sure that Sandy was gone, but then she spotted a wonderfully familiar sight. Sandy was there after all!

Next to Sandy, wobbling on spindly legs, was the cutest foal Alice had ever seen. It looked identical to Sandy. "What a wonderful surprise," said Alice, happily. Now she would have to spend even more time at the farm.

Abigail's Perfect Pet

Abigail wanted a pet of her own more than anything else in the whole world. She'd begged her parents for a dog or cat, but they'd always said no. "They need feeding, grooming and taking to the vet," Dad pointed out.

"You're not big enough just yet," added Mum. "Maybe when you're a bit older."

Then, one day, Mum and Abigail were walking home when they bumped into their neighbour walking her dog.

"Poor Digby hasn't had much exercise lately because of my bad leg," said Mrs Brown.

"Abigail could walk him for you," said Mum. "She loves dogs." So, the next day, Abigail set off for the park with Digby.

"Looking after a dog is easy," said Abigail, as she and Digby strolled through the park, Digby sniffing at the piles of leaves. Suddenly, with an excited bark, Digby caught sight of a ball and dashed off after it, splashing through a muddy stream and up a slippery bank. "Stop, Digby!" cried Abigail, but it was no good. Digby just kept running.

Abigail ran after Digby, but he ran even faster. Before long, he reached the woods at the top of a hill. Abigail ran behind him, calling his name. Then she remembered what Mrs Brown had said about Digby loving treats, so Abigail dug her hand into her pocket, pulling out a bone-shaped biscuit.

By the time she caught Digby and got home, Abigail was worn out and she looked a mess. "Digby took me for a walk," Abigail said to her mum, who grinned when she saw her.
"It looks like you both got plenty of exercise," said Mum, laughing and looking down at Digby who'd fallen asleep at her feet.

"You're right, Mum," said Abigail. "Looking after a pet is hard work."

A few days later, Abigail got a big surprise. She found a glass bowl with a shiny goldfish swimming around inside.
"He'll be easier to look after than a dog," said Dad.
"We know you'll look after him," added Mum.
"He's the perfect pet," said Abigail, smiling.

The Fairy Night Owl

"I've had a lovely day," sighed Faye the fairy to her family. As the daylight faded and night began to fill the sky, she was walking home with her mum, dad and little sister. They were looking up at the sky, but Faye was watching the dark shadows. "I don't like the dark," whispered Faye, squeezing Dad's hand, tightly. "It's scary."

"No it isn't," said a friendly voice above them. It was a white owl in a tree. "I'm the fairy night owl," she said, hooting gently. "I want to show you how wonderful the night-time can be."

The fairy night owl explained that when the sun goes down,
the moon and stars come out. "Sometimes you will see fireflies,
too," she said. Dad pointed up to the sky and Faye gasped.
"I can see the moon and stars and fireflies. They are so bright."

"Let me show you the moon flowers," said the owl. She took everyone to a patch of flowers that glowed like lights. "They only glow bright in the dark of the night," said the owl. Faye picked some of the flowers.

"They will light our way home!" she cried.

With the magical flowers and the light of the stars and moon, Faye and her family were soon back home. Mum suggested they make a decoration using the moon flowers. "We'll hang it in your room," said Dad, smiling. "It will glow all night and you won't be afraid."

Soon, it was time for Faye to go to bed. Dad hung up her enchanted light and tucked her in. Outside, the night owl hooted. "Thank you, Night Owl," said Faye. "Now I know how magical the night can be, I will never be afraid again." With that, she felt fast asleep.

The Secret Door

Mum, Dad, Jake and Alana were visiting Craggy Castle for a day out. Dad had been looking at the guide book. "There's a secret passage in the castle," he said. "I hope we find it."

Across the hallway, Alana was looking at a tapestry on the wall which showed an old castle surrounded by rolling hills. She suddenly heard a strange noise and leaned closer. She heard it again. A deep rumbling came from behind the tapestry. Peeling the material back, Alana discovered an old door. She opened it and slipped through.

Alana found she had stepped into a strange land where a princess lived. The princess didn't look very happy. "Are you here to get rid of the dragon?" she asked, hopefully. "He roars all day and night. Everyone is terrified."

In the distance there was a loud rumble and a noisy growl. "That's him now," said the princess, pointing upwards.

Alana looked up and saw a huge dragon flying towards them. Smoke came from his nostrils and his long tail lashed around. However, as he flew closer, Alana noticed that the noise wasn't a roar, but a rumble. "His tummy's rumbling," she said. "He's hungry." She took a sandwich from her backpack and offered it to the dragon.

The dragon took the sandwich from Alana's hand and swallowed it. Then, he ate the rest of her lunch. "We need more food," said Alana. The princess told the castle cooks and they made a huge pot of stew which Alana and the princess gave to the dragon. He ate it hungrily, gave a small burp and flew away.

"You will be my guest of honour at a special banquet,"
the princess told Alana. "You're so brave."
"Thank you," said Alana, "but I have to get back to my family."
They said goodbye and, checking that no one was watching,
Alana slipped through the secret doorway and back into the
corridor, just as her family were approaching.

Heading for the exit, they passed the tapestry once more and Alana noticed it had changed. As well as the castle and hills, it now showed the dragon too, complete with a big, fat stomach. She also saw two girls on a tower pulling up an empty stew pot. "That must be me and the princess," she thought, smiling.

"So, has everyone had fun?" asked Dad, as they continued along the corridor. Suddenly, there was a low growling sound. "What's that noise?" asked Mum, looking around.

"It's my stomach," Alana admitted. As they headed out of the castle, Alana whispered to Jake, "If you share your sandwiches with me, I'll tell you an amazing story."